THE STORY OF
MAY

THE STORY OF
MAY

by MORDICAI GERSTEIN

HarperCollins*Publishers*

Poem #1768 is reprinted by permission of the publishers
and the Trustees of Amherst College from
The Poems of Emily Dickinson, Thomas H. Johnson, ed.,
Cambridge, Mass.: The Belknap Press of Harvard University Press,
Copyright © 1951, 1955, 1979, 1983 by the President
and Fellows of Harvard College.

Library of Congress Cataloging-in-Publication Data
Gerstein, Mordicai.
    The story of May / by Mordicai Gerstein.
        p.   cm.
    Summary: The month of May travels to meet her father,
December, and meets all of her relatives, the other months of the
year, on the way.
    ISBN 0-06-022288-3.—ISBN 0-06-022289-1 (lib. bdg.)
    [1. Months—Fiction.]
PZ7.G325St 1993   90-22410
[E]—dc20   CIP
                                       AC

Typography by Christine Kettner
1 2 3 4 5 6 7 8 9 10
First Edition

For Jesse Gerstein

September 4, 1957–October 14, 1991

...faithful be
To Thyself,
And Mystery—
All the rest is Perjury—

—*Emily Dickinson*

APRIL AND MAY

"LITTLE MAY," said April softly, "wake up. Today is special!"

It wasn't quite dawn. The month of May stretched and rubbed her eyes. She was just a little girl, much younger than she is now.

"It's still dark," she said, yawning.

"My dear," said her mother, "there are certain things a young spring month is expected to do. Today I'm going to show you what they are."

"Hooray!" cried May, and jumped out of bed.

Usually, April was full of jokes and giggles, but not today. Patiently, she showed May how to scatter wildflowers, how to welcome returning birds, and how to make cherry and apple buds swell and blossom.

May thought everything April did was wonderful. She watched with wide eyes, and after an hour or two and a little practice, she said, "Mother, I'm ready to do it myself."

She looked so eager, with flower-tangled hair and muddy feet, that April had to laugh and hug her.

"All right," said April, "but don't go off too far, and be home in time for supper."

May skipped into the morning. She sprinkled periwinkles at the edges of woods. She spun round and round, tossing dandelions, bluets and violets everywhere. She welcomed the warblers and listened to their gossip of foreign places. She wandered farther, and she didn't notice the trees becoming greener and the sun becoming warmer. Suddenly, she stopped and looked around.

The air was full of falling petals, and the dandelions had turned to fluff and were blowing away. There were flowers she didn't know, and everything looked strange. She was lost.

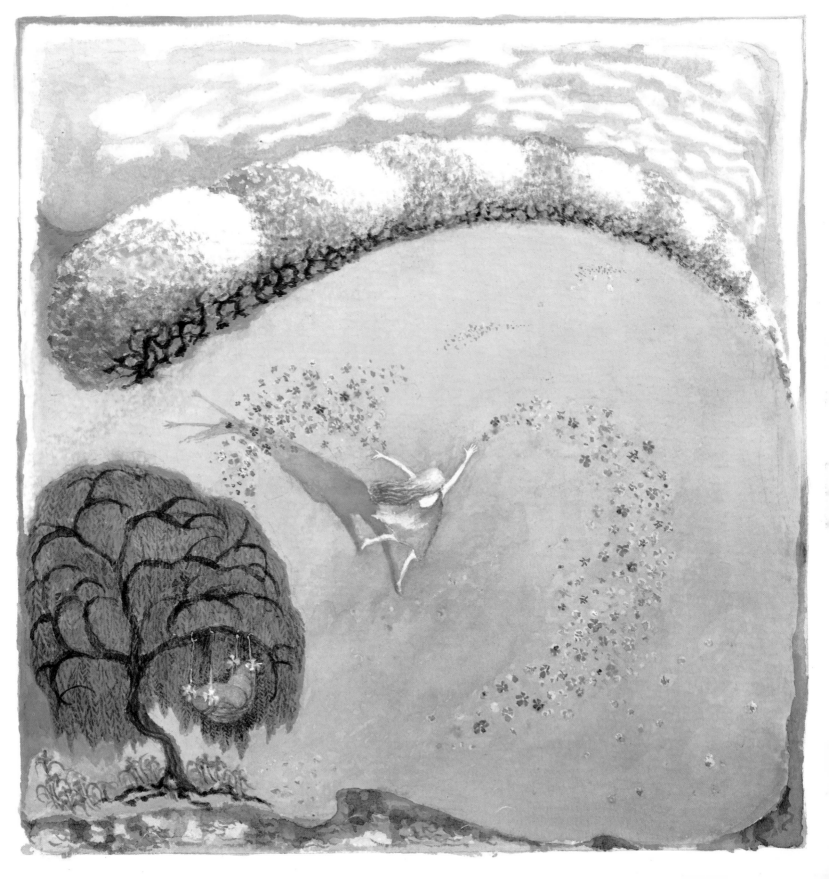

JUNE

"MAY!" said a voice that made her jump. "I know it's you, though I haven't seen you since you were born. I'm your aunt June."

May looked up at a brown-armed woman with a wheelbarrow. Her green-velvet dress had countless pockets, all full of seed packages and twittering baby birds.

"What are you doing so far from home?" she asked May. "Are you going to visit your father?"

"My father?" said May. "Do I have a father?" Her mother had never mentioned one, and being so young, May had never thought to ask.

"Who is he? Where does he live?"

"Maybe I shouldn't have said anything," said June uneasily.

"Please tell me," insisted May. "I should know who my father is."

"Well, all I know," said June, "is that he lives off at the other end of the year somewhere."

"Where is that?"

"It's over those fields and woods, and then over the hills and mountains beyond. Very far and very cold."

"COLD?...What is that?"

"That's when the sun doesn't warm you, and nothing grows, and the whole world is white."

"How awful!" said May with a shudder.

"Oh, never mind," said June. "Come! See my garden."

Bordered with irises and tulips, the garden was full of the sprouts and vines of every kind of flower and vegetable.

"Some say vegetables must be eaten as soon as they're picked," said June. "But the deer and rabbits taught me to eat them *before*

they're picked." She and May sat in the middle of the garden nibbling snow peas off the vine, and lettuce and beet greens right from the rows. Two rabbits and a fawn ate with them.

"Thank you, Aunt June, for the lovely lunch," said May. "I'm going to visit my father now."

June looked worried. "Do take care," she called, as May hurried up a grassy hill.

JULY

MAY COULD HEAR music, and as she climbed, it became louder and wilder. At the top, in the middle of a field of young corn, she saw an immense, red-faced man in overalls. He sang loudly, and with a hoe he conducted an orchestra of katydids, bees, crickets, and birds. Buzzing, chirping, and warbling, they swarmed around his huge straw hat.

"May!" he shouted through the din. "Gosh, you've grown! Do you like our song? I call it 'A Summer Day.'"

"I've never heard anything like it," said May.

"Why, thank you. Let's have a snack and go for a swim. I'm your uncle July."

Singing with May on his shoulder and a gigantic green watermelon under his arm, July made his way out of the field down to a wide, sandy beach.

"What's that?" asked May, pointing to the ocean. July laughed and set her down on the smooth wet sand. The foamy surf tickled May's toes like kittens' tongues. July showed her how to float and swim. Then May and her uncle sat in the sun, eating watermelon and spitting seeds into the sea.

"I'm going to visit my father," said May. "Do you know where he lives?"

"Hmmm. Not exactly," said July. "It's over the sea somewhere—
very far and very cold." He shivered and waved toward the horizon.
"How can I get over the sea?" asked May. "It looks endless."

"I think your grandfather can help you with that," said July.
"Look there!" He lifted May to the top of a grassy dune.

AUGUST

ON THE OTHER side of the dune lay a man that shone like a hill of polished copper. His snoring sounded like pebbles in the surf. A rainbow-colored sailboat sat beside him.

"Wake up!" shouted July. "Meet your pretty granddaughter." He stood May on the man's belly. "May, this is your grandpa August."

August yawned and smiled up at her with coppery eyes. "Would you like a boat ride?" he asked. His voice was like molasses, deep and slow.

"I would," May answered. "Thank you." July chuckled as he pushed the boat into the surf and helped them into it. The sails flapped at first, then filled and creaked.

"Sweet sailing!" July sang from the shore.

The water was calm and greeny-blue, and the ship moved swiftly. May looked down and saw all the creatures of the sea.

"There's an octopus," said her grandfather, "and that one's a jellyfish..."

When night came, he showed her animal pictures in the stars. As the stars faded and August snored, May saw the sun peek over the horizon. Then she saw another sun, and another, till hundreds of suns blazed into the dawn.

SEPTEMBER

"THOSE ARE SUNFLOWERS," yawned August, "and this is as far as I go." The boat gently bumped an old wooden pier. August set May on it and left her with a warm kiss and a pocketful of shells.

The pier was piled with baskets of fruit and vegetables. A sign said:

HELP YOURSELF! PLEASE! THERE'S MORE!

The sunflowers blazed against the deep-blue sky, but something in the air made May shiver. The light was more transparent, and the crickets sang more slowly. Beyond the sunflowers she found a golden woman surrounded by hills of tomatoes, squash, and peppers, and mountains of pumpkins.

"May!" she called. "Come help with the harvest. I'm your aunt September." She put wreaths of onions around May's neck.

"When we were children, your father and I played together. The world was still new. There were no rules yet, and we months wandered as we pleased. It was because of your parents that we settled into the places we have now. Your father settled in the northernmost mountains of the year, just beyond the orchards of his brother, October. Come, take more tomatoes and peppers, and a pumpkin for October. I'll show you the path."

OCTOBER

THE PATH was lined with piled stones covered with vines of purple grapes. As May walked, leaves began to fall around her. She was amazed to see that they were gold, crimson, orange, purple—anything but green. The wind whirled the leaves into the sky, and all around she heard the soft thumps of apples falling.

"Watch out below!" a voice sang out. May ducked her head, and a dozen apples bounced around her. She looked up. There was October in an apple tree. His cape and clothes were a patchwork of colored leaves, and his red hair and beard fluttered like flames in the wind. He leaped and landed in front of May with a bow.

"My name is May," she said. "I've brought you a pumpkin."

"Why, it's magnificent!" said October, holding up the pumpkin. "Don't move! I shall carve your pumpkin portrait!"

May sat as still as she could while October squinted at her, and started to carve the pumpkin with a large pocketknife. He whistled as he worked.

"Now, let's have a big smile," he said. May smiled. "Bigger!" said October. May's cheeks ached, and chunks of pumpkin flew in all directions.

"There! It's a perfect likeness, don't you think?" He held up the pumpkin, and May tried not to laugh.

"It's very nice," she giggled politely, though she had never seen anything so funny-looking.

October bowed and winked. "Now, have an apple and come with me. Your father can't wait to see you.

"Make way! Make way!" he shouted. A crowd of porcupines and groundhogs had gathered, all munching September's vegetables and October's apples.

"Nothing goes to waste here," said October.

"Are we almost where my father lives?" May asked.

"Not far," said October. "We're brothers, you know, but we're completely different. I love all the colors; he cares for only one."

"Which one?" asked May.

"White," said October. "That house up the hill is our mother's. She's your grandmother. She'll take you to your father."

The wind was becoming colder and stronger. October wrapped his cloak around May, and with a crisp kiss, he sent her up the hill.

NOVEMBER

MAY KNOCKED at the door of the small gray house. The sun was melting into the mountains, and huge, black storm clouds boiled overhead. On the barren hillside, gray grasses hissed and whispered in the chill wind.

The woman who opened the door embraced May. "Come in where it's cozy!" she said. "I'm your grandmother November."

In her soft gray gown she was no taller than May, and her rosy cheeks were wrinkled as old apples.

"Sit by the stove and I'll heat some cider." The house was fragrant with cinnamon and nutmeg, and the stove glowed and crackled. The corners of the room were full of shadows and shelves of preserves. May had never been in a house before.

As the wind moaned and banged a shutter, they sipped hot spiced cider and ate warm gingerbread, and May told November all about springtime.

"Goodness gracious! It sounds wonderful!" said her grandmother. "And now if you're ready, I'll take you to your father. He'll be thrilled to see you."

They went out the back door into a rattling field of dried cornstalks. In the failing light, rows of dead sunflowers hung their

great heads and swayed and sighed. May had never seen dead things before. She had never felt cold. She held November's hand tightly. Something white whirled through the air and touched May's face with icy sparks.

"It's snow," said November. "You'll see lots of it here." The snow grew thicker. She gripped November's hand, but as they

struggled against the fierce wind, her grandmother's hand slipped from hers.

"November!" May cried. "November!" But the wind cried louder and blew her words away.

DECEMBER

ALONE, MAY stumbled through the howling darkness. Suddenly a door opened in front of her. Light and warmth blazed out and a tall figure reached down for her.

"My dear, dear daughter," said a sweet rumbling voice. "I am your father. December is my name."

His hair and beard were white and soft as the fleece he wore. He carried May into a palace of ice, down halls where fragrant balsam and cedar trees grew. In front of a blazing fireplace carved from a glacier, he set her down and gave her a hot mug of something that smelled wonderful.

"It's called cocoa," said her father. "I just want to look at you.... Yes! You have your mother's smile." He watched her for a long time, then looked into the fire and began to speak.

"I met your mother long ago, back when we months wandered free. I loved her smile and her sense of humor. She'd spread sunshine all over, and when everyone came out to play, she'd suddenly drench them with buckets of sleet and hail. I was the only one who thought she was funny. We married right away, but there was trouble from the start.

"I'd coat the trees with gorgeous ice, not noticing your mother had sewn new leaves on them. She'd have a fit and turn everything

to mud. Or she would invite the birds to visit, and I'd whip up a blizzard. The poor things would have to fly off to find June or August. We had terrible fights; ice storms and sun showers. The other months were in a state of nervous confusion. Finally, the

family decided we should all settle into some sensible order, and your mother and I were put at opposite ends of the year. And you are our daughter, the loveliest month of all.''

That night, May slept under fat down quilts, and in the morning she looked out at a world of dazzling white. Outside in the fresh-fallen snow, bird and animal tracks looked like printing on a page. May and her father built a snowman and pelted him with snowballs. They sledded down endless hills, and the days and weeks passed quickly.

But one morning May woke up and thought she heard April's voice in the wind. She tried to remember how a daffodil smelled, but she couldn't.

"I think I should go home now," she said to her father. "My mother might be worried."

Her father looked sad. "Will you come back and visit again?"

"Oh yes," said May. "I love being here with you!"

Her father beamed. "All right," he said. "My brother January will take you home."

"But shouldn't I go back to Grandmother November?"

"No," said December, "the world is round, and so is time. If you go on, you'll get back to where you started." May's father hugged her and kissed her good-bye. "Give my love to your mother," he said.

JANUARY

UNCLE JANUARY picked May up and wrapped her in his dark woolen cloak. Then they were flying down the mountain, swerving right and left around snow-crusted pines.

"Do you have wings?" asked May.

"No!" laughed her uncle. "I have skis!" January's smile sparkled like the snow, and his curly black hair bounced when he laughed.

They swooped through snowy valleys where chickadees whistled, and on the shore of a frozen lake they saw an igloo and stopped.

"Hey! Sister!" January called. "Our niece, May, is here. She needs to cross your lake."

FEBRUARY

THERE WAS A SNEEZE from the igloo. A round rumpled face with watery eyes and a red nose poked out the door and sniffled.

"I've got a cold," said February sadly.

January laughed. "You've always got a cold. But hurry! May's mother is waiting for her."

February crawled out and blew her nose. She looked like a bag of rags. Over layers of shirts and sweaters she wore dozens of mufflers; May couldn't count all her hats.

"Glad to beet you, Bay," said February. She helped May lace on a pair of silver ice skates, then took her hand and off they skated, leaving January laughing on the shore.

February sniffled and sneezed while she whirled over the ice doing figure eights. Then May heard a creaking sound and saw the ice begin to crack.

"Oh MY!" cried February. "We've reached the thaw!" The ice broke into bobbing chunks. May almost slipped into the rushing water, but February caught her.

"OH DEAR!" February moaned and sneezed as their piece of ice moved faster and faster and became smaller and smaller. May could hear a roaring sound ahead.

"It's the Ides!" wailed February. "March!" she called. "Where are you?"

"Are you calling my cousin March?" asked May.

"Yes!" sniffled February. "He's my son, and he better get here quick! The Ides are rocky falls ahead. After them, it's all downhill till spring!"

MARCH

"HALLOO!" boomed a voice out of the wind. May saw her cousin March swoop down to them. He was strapped to a great silver-and-blue kite, and his shaggy head bristled with icicles. He took May under one arm and his mother under the other, and they were in the sky above the falls before May could catch her breath.

"Where were you?" scolded February, blowing her nose.

"Gathering the winds, Mother!" roared March. "Gathering them into a gale to fly my kite on!" His laugh blew them higher. Then, gently kissing May's cheek, he whispered, "We missed you."

He flew back upriver to where the ice was solid and set his mother down on her skates.

"Thank goodness!" she sniffled. "Now just wait a minute...." She dug around under her sweaters and mufflers till she found a big red envelope.

"This is for you, May. Good-bye!" She skated off in a flurry of sneezes as May opened the envelope. It was a big red, heart-shaped card, all lined with lace and ribbon. *I love you, May* was written in the middle.

"She gives them to everyone," laughed March, leaping with May into the sky.

APRIL

BENEATH THEM, the earth was turning a soft green. They floated lower as the winds died, and then, below them, May saw her mother looking very tiny. She was waving.

May bounced onto the grass and leaped into her mother's arms.

"Welcome home, my baby!" said April. "I missed you so!"

March giggled and his icicles melted, and as they all had supper, May told of her travels.

"…and your father, is he well?" asked April.

"Yes," said May, "and he sends you his love."

"Humph!" said her mother.

MAY VISITED her father often, and from time to time, she still does. If you feel a warm breeze on a December day, or think you hear a robin, it's almost certain May is there. Or if a blizzard hits in the middle of April, you can guess that December stopped in to say hello.

But most of the time, the months stay where they belong. And because the earth is round and always turning, we visit each of the months every year, year after year, the way one does with family, or dear old friends.

The text for Mordicai Gerstein's *The Story of May* was composed in
Gallia and Horley Old Style Light by Cardinal Communications Group.
The paintings were executed with Winsor & Newton transparent watercolors
on Arches watercolor paper.
The color separations were made by Bright Arts/Hong Kong.
Production by Erin Dwyer.
Typography by Christine Kettner.